This
Ready Steady Read
book belongs to:

My Reading Tree!

KT-424-796

For Dave
~ A.H.B.

For Jamie and Joseph
~ G.W.

LITTLE TIGER PRESS
An imprint of Magi Publications
1 The Coda Centre, 189 Munster Road, London SW6 6AW
www.littletigerpress.com
First published in Great Britain 2000
This edition published 2009
Text copyright © A. H. Benjamin 2000
Illustrations copyright © Gwyneth Williamson 2000
A. H. Benjamin and Gwyneth Williamson have asserted their
rights to be identified as the author and illustrator of this work
under the Copyright, Designs and Patents Act, 1988
All rights reserved • ISBN 978-1-84506-878-3
Printed in China
2 4 6 8 10 9 7 5 3 1

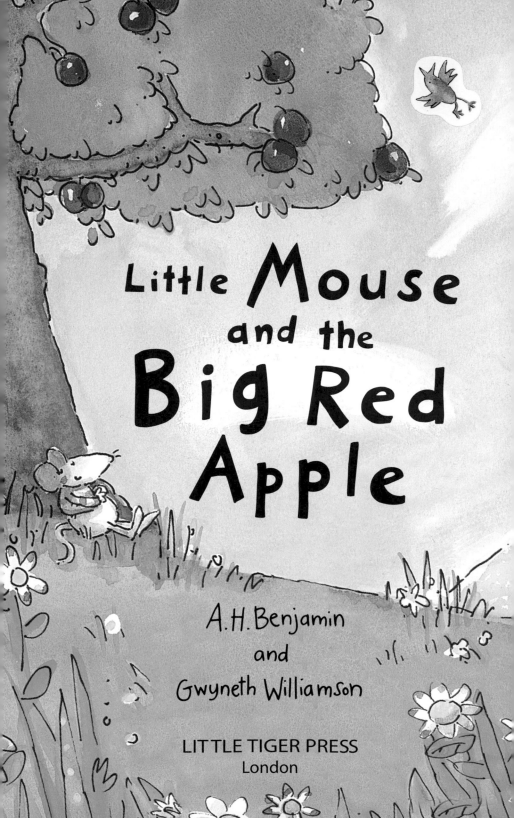

Little Mouse and the Big Red Apple

A. H. Benjamin

and

Gwyneth Williamson

LITTLE TIGER PRESS
London

Mouse was feeling a bit peckish
one day when all of a sudden he
came across a big, red, juicy apple.
"Just what I fancy!" he cried.
"I'll take it home with me and
have a feast!"

Mouse set off towards his little house,
rolling the apple over and over.

He couldn't wait to get his teeth into
the big, red, juicy apple. "Yum, yum,"
he thought, when all of a sudden . . .

SPLASH!

. . . the apple rolled into a pond.

"Oh no!" wailed Mouse. "What am I going to do now?"

"Not to worry," said Frog, hopping out of the water. "I'll help you."

Frog kicked the apple hard with his strong
back legs. It flew out of the water, and . . .

BUMP!

landed on the ground.

"There you are," said Frog. He licked
his lips and stared at the apple.
   "Er, thanks," said Mouse, as he began to
roll it along the path. He did not want
to share his apple with Frog.

Mouse went on his way, thinking of the
lovely apple dinner he would have later.
His mouth was already watering when . . .

the big, red,
juicy apple
fell into a
thorn bush.

"Silly me!"
muttered Mouse,
as he tried to
rescue his dinner.
"Ouch, that hurt!"
he cried. "Those
prickles are nasty!"

"I see you have a problem,"
said Tortoise, trundling up
to Mouse. "Leave it to me."
    Tortoise didn't have to worry
about the sharp prickles. He
had his shell to protect him.

Without any trouble at all, Tortoise
crept under the thorn bush and brought
out the big, red, juicy apple.

"Problem solved!" he said, stroking
the apple longingly.

"I'm ever so grateful," said Mouse
in a hurried voice, and he was off
again. He did not want to share
his apple with Tortoise.

"I'll soon be home and tucking
into that big, red, juicy apple,"
thought Mouse, when . . .

. . . the apple rolled into a log.
"That's all I need!" sighed Mouse
when he saw that the log blocked
his path. "How do I get round that?"

"Easy!" said Mole, popping out of
a nearby hole. "I'll dig you a tunnel."
And she did. She dug a tunnel that
went right under the log.

It was just wide enough for Mouse
and the apple to go through it.
  "Always glad to help!" said Mole,
sniffing at the big, red, juicy apple
with her little nose.

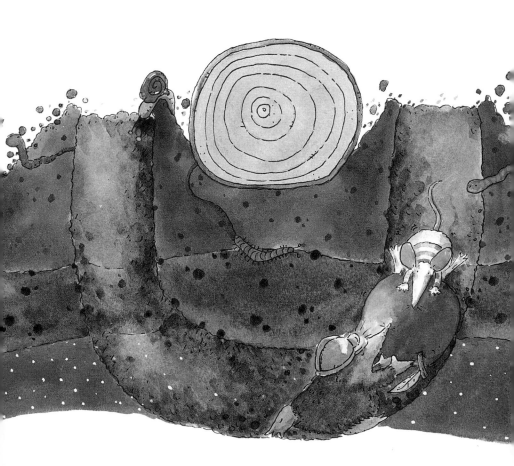

"It's very kind of you," said Mouse,
and he went on his way as fast as
he could. He did not want to share
the apple with Mole.

He rolled the apple over and
over until . . .

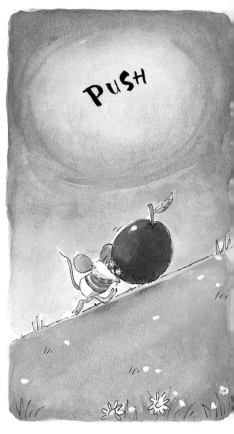

. . . he came to
a steep hill.
His house was
at the very top.

Push, push,
heave, heave,
went Mouse,
grunting and
groaning.

Up, up, up
he went, until
he reached the
very top.

"At last!" sighed
Mouse happily.
"Oh for that lovely
apple meal!" But,
as Mouse let go . . .

. . . the apple wobbled,
and then it started to roll
down the other side of
the hill!

It rolled
faster and
faster . . .

further
and further,
until . . .

. . . it came to a stop
at the bottom of the hill.
Mouse could see it lying there,
like a big, red jewel.

"Oh no," he cried, "I shall
have to start all over again!"

Mouse scrabbled down the
hill on his little tired feet.

Faster and faster he ran.
But when he reached the bottom . . .

. . . he found Frog, Mole and Tortoise
had got there first!

"How kind of you to send that apple
all the way back to us," called out
Mole, chomping away on a piece of it.

Mouse gave a big, big sigh.
"Don't mention it," he said.
"Isn't that what friends are for?"

Picture Dictionary

Look at the words below and put the correct picture stickers next to each word.

frog

apple

tree

bird

Have you got these right?
Then put a star on your reading tree!

Amazing Alphabet

a b c d e f g h i j k l m n
o p q r s t u v w x y z

Put the word stickers in the right alphabetical order, using the alphabet above to help.

log – dinner – tunnel – pond – bush – hill

1) _____   2) _____   3) _____

4) _____   5) _____   6) _____

Did you get this right?
Add another star to your reading tree!

Cool Vowels and Consonants

The alphabet is made up of vowels and consonants.

Vowels sound soft. They are: a e i o u.

Consonants sound harder. They are:
b c d f g h j k l m n p q r s t v w x y z.

1) Circle the words that begin with a vowel.

over	feast	apple
shell	up	red

2) Circle the words that begin with a consonant.

share	off	out
thorn	until	bush

3) Circle the words that begin with a consonant
and end with a vowel.

mouse	sudden	voice
home	thought	legs

4) Circle the words that begin with a vowel
and end with a consonant.

under	fast	again
happily	ouch	wide

  Did you spot the vowels and consonants?
Add a star to your reading tree!

Awesome Adjectives

An **adjective** is a describing word. Add the missing adjectives to the sentences from the story below using the word stickers.

tired – red – little – juicy – big

1) Mouse set off towards his _____ house, rolling the apple over and over.

2) He couldn't wait to get his teeth into the big, red, _____ apple.

3) Mouse could see it lying there, like a big, _____ jewel.

4) Mouse scrabbled down the hill on his little _____ feet.

5) Mouse gave a _____ , big sigh.

 Did you get all the adjectives right? Great! Add another star to your reading tree.

Cool Questions

Some sentences are questions.
You know when a sentence is a question because
it has a **question mark** (?) at the end of it.

Put a **question mark** at the end of the sentences that
are questions. Put a **full stop** at the end of the
sentences that are not questions.

1) What am I going to do now

2) I'll help you

3) How do I get round that

4) His house was at the very top

5) Isn't that what friends are for

 Did you get these right?
Remember to add another
star to your reading tree!

Same Meanings

Match the words on the left to the words on the right that have the same meaning. We've done the first one for you.

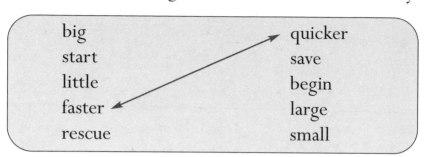

big   quicker
start   save
little   begin
faster   large
rescue   small

Did you match the words?
Add another star to your reading tree.

Busy Verbs

A **verb** is a doing word. Add the missing verbs from the **Busy Verbs** stickers to these sentences from the story.

share – licked – scrabbled – rolled

1) He _____ his lips and stared at the apple.

2) He did not want to _____ his apple with Tortoise.

3) He _____ the apple over and over until . . .

4) Mouse _____ down the hill on his little tired feet.

Did you get all the verbs right? Great!
Add the last star to your reading tree!